Giada De Laurentiis's

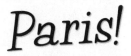

Recipe for Adventure

Paris!

written with Taylor Morris
illustrated by Francesca Gambatesa

Grosset & Dunlap
An Imprint of Penguin Group (USA)

To my sweet Jade and all the children who dream of the painted skies
and chocolate croissants of beautiful Paris!

Pour ma douce Jade et tous les enfants qui rêvent des cieux peints
et des pains au chocolat de la belle ville de Paris!

GROSSET & DUNLAP
Published by the Penguin Group
Penguin Group (USA) Inc., 375 Hudson Street, New York, New York 10014, USA

USA | Canada | UK | Ireland | Australia | New Zealand | India | South Africa | China
Penguin Books Ltd, Registered Offices: 80 Strand, London WC2R 0RL, England

For more information about the Penguin Group visit penguin.com

Text copyright © 2013 by GDL Foods, Inc. Illustrations copyright © 2013 by Francesca Gambatesa.
Published by Grosset & Dunlap, a division of Penguin Young Readers Group, 345 Hudson Street, New York, New York 10014.
GROSSET & DUNLAP is a trademark of Penguin Group (USA) Inc. Printed in the U.S.A.

ISBN 978-0-448-46257-8 (pb)   10 9 8 7 6 5 4 3 2 1
ISBN 978-0-448-47854-8 (hc)   10 9 8 7 6 5 4 3 2 1

Chapter 1

All Alfie could see was the goal. With each step he guided the ball toward the net, where a frightened-looking Jackson stood guard.

Quick as a cheetah, Alfie dodged the other players. From the corner of his eye he saw people shouting and waving their hands, but he tuned it all out and kept his focus steady. He aimed. He kicked. The ball sailed past Jackson, who reacted so slowly that he didn't even raise his hands to block the ball until it was already bouncing in the corner of the net. Victory was Alfie's.

"Yes! In your face, Jackson!"

Alfie ran screaming across the soccer field while

the other team—which was really part of his own team, since this was a practice game—looked away, probably ashamed of their own performance.

"Bertolizzi!" Coach Schrader called from the sidelines. "Get over here!"

Alfie ran toward Coach feeling as if he'd found his place in life. This was the first year he'd played a sport in the after-school program, and it was turning out to be the best decision of his ten-year-old life. In fact, Coach was probably about to make him team captain!

However, Coach Schrader's face looked a little red, like *he'd* been the one racing across the field toward total domination.

"What was that?" Coach asked, gesturing toward the field.

"A goal, sir. A point for my team."

"Your team?"

"Well, the jerseys." He tugged on the yellow jersey his side wore for the practice game.

"Alfredo," said Coach. He rarely called the kids by their first names, and he had never called Alfie by his proper name. "You had shirts all over you. Didn't you see?"

"Yes, sir," he said, because of course he'd seen. He'd seen and he'd conquered!

"If you saw, then why didn't you pass?"

"Pass?"

"The ball, Bertolizzi. Why didn't you pass the ball? You had two teammates in the clear."

"Coach . . . ," Alfie said. Clearly the guy was confused. "I got the goal. My team won. Isn't that the whole point?"

"Is that what you think?" his coach asked.

Alfie was positive this was a trick question. Of course he knew that winning was the point—they weren't out here to just kick the ball back and forth—but he got the feeling he couldn't say that out loud. So he said, "No, sir," even though he really wanted to say, "Well, yeah. Duh!"

Alfie was 100 percent positive you couldn't say *duh* to your coach.

"We have our first game on Saturday," Coach said, as if Alfie needed reminding. He couldn't wait! "I need players on the

field who are a part of a team. Not some one-man show."

"I'm ready to play, Coach."

"I know you can play, but can you play on a team?" he said. "'In your face'? Really?"

Alfie suddenly became very aware of his surroundings. The other players were standing on the field not too far from them. Coach wasn't yelling at Alfie, but Alfie was sure those kids could hear every word. Even worse, some kids—including a few girls from his class—were sitting in the bleachers doing homework and watching practice.

"There's nothing worse than an obnoxious winner," Coach said. "Until you can be a respectful team player, I'm going to have to bench you for Saturday's game."

"But, Coach!"

"I'm sorry, Alfie. I've made my decision."

"How am I supposed to learn to be a team player when I'm sitting on the bench?" Alfie asked desperately. It didn't even make sense!

"Hopefully you'll figure that out," Coach said. "I expect you to be here suited up at every practice, on time with the rest of your team."

"Suit up to do nothing? No thanks," he said.

"I'll tell you this once," Coach Schrader said, lowering his voice. "If you're not at the game on Saturday, supporting your team, then you're off the team. Is that clear?"

"Yes, sir," Alfie muttered.

The last thing he wanted was to get kicked off the team. But sitting on the bench the whole game? That was just about the worst thing that could happen.

Chapter 2

"Should I order pizza from Presto Pesto for dinner?" Zia Donatella asked that night.

"Zia!" said Emilia, Alfie's sister. She was older than him by one year, but sometimes she acted like a thirty-year-old. "You hate Presto Pesto."

"I don't *hate* anything, and neither should you," Zia said. Her long salt-and-pepper hair was pulled back in a braid, and the faded, fitted jeans she wore looked straight out of a Western movie. *A* spaghetti *Western*, thought Alfie.

"Well, I don't want it," Emilia said. "I'd rather you make a pizza from scratch."

"Oh, really!" Zia laughed, touching her stone necklace as she did. Zia had all sorts of trinkets from her travels around the world. Those stones just might be from ancient Egypt. "You think I can just whip up a homemade pizza like that?"

"Leave her alone, Emilia," Alfie said. "We can order in if you want, Zia."

Alfie only said this because Emilia was getting on his nerves. Everyone was getting on his nerves, except for Zia. As soon as he'd gotten home from school, his mom demanded he clean up the study, where he was sleeping while Zia stayed in his room. Then when his dad got home, he told Alfie he needed to take out the trash. Everyone was on his case today.

"Oh, kids, I'm teasing," Zia said. "No pizza tonight. I'm cooking you something new."

"When you say *new*," Alfie said, "what exactly do you mean?"

The first time Zia had cooked for them, something

utterly impossible had happened. As she made them an Italian treat called *zeppole*, she told Alfie and Emilia about growing up in Naples, Italy, and how she would always buy a warm, freshly made zeppole any time she had a little pocket money. When Alfie and Emilia bit into the fluffy fried treat, they were transported—literally!—to Naples. They spent an entire day there with a boy named Marco, whose family made the best pizza in all of Naples. They even won the top prize at the city's annual pizza festival.

So now that Zia had that look in her eyes and said she was going to cook "something new," Alfie and Emilia became suspicious.

"Let me go pack a bag," Alfie said. Maybe if they went to Naples again—and he hoped they would—he could be better prepared.

"No. State qui ed aiutami!" Zia said. "Stay and help. The food is always better when you cook together."

Mom ruffled Alfie's hair as she walked by him, and

he pulled away. "Wow! Someone's grumpy."

"I'm not grumpy," Alfie said, even though he totally was. How could he not be after the way he was treated today?

Mom washed her hands. As she dried them on a towel, she went to the refrigerator. Meanwhile, Zia drizzled olive oil in a pan and turned on the burner.

"Bad day at school?" Mom asked.

"Is there ever a good day at school?" Alfie said.

"Watch the attitude," Mom said, her arms loaded with fresh vegetables.

The last thing Alfie needed was to get in trouble, so instead of being mad, he decided to tell everyone what was wrong.

"School was okay," Alfie said. "Soccer practice was a beating."

"I thought you said you were going to be the big star on the team, captain and everything," Emilia said with a smirk.

"I am, and I will be," he said defiantly. "It's just that Coach wants to give some of the other players a chance to play, so he's thinking of sitting me out for Saturday's game."

"So, wait," Emilia said. "You're telling us that you got benched for being *too good*?"

"Basically," Alfie said.

"Sure." Emilia laughed. "Keep telling yourself that."

"Could you stop talking, please?"

"Kids," Mom warned.

"I said please," Alfie said.

"We'll come to your game no matter what," Mom said. "You're on the team, and we support you."

"What's this?" Zia said, inspecting Mom's ingredients. "Red pepper flakes? That's not how we make spaghetti in Naples."

"A little heat changes it up. It's okay to do things differently sometimes. Alfie, why don't you cut up that carrot for the salad?" She pointed to the counter.

"It's just that I've been working really hard," Alfie continued. "When I'm on the soccer field I feel like . . . I don't know. Like I'm really good at something."

"You're good at lots of things," Zia said. "Your sense of

direction is *molto buono*, and you know more about maps and geography than any other ten-year-old I know."

"But if you're sitting on the bench you won't be going anywhere," Emilia said with a laugh.

"Mom!" Alfie snapped. "Would you tell her to stop?"

"It's a joke," Emilia said. "Get a sense of humor."

"I mean it, you two," Mom said, pointing the knife she was using to slice an onion.

Emilia went around to Mom's side of the counter and got a smaller knife out of the drawer. "I'll slice the carrots," she said, and Alfie had to bite his tongue to stop himself from calling her a goody-goody.

"Careful with the knife," Mom said, watching her closely.

Emilia began cutting the carrots at an angle like Zia had taught her, while Alfie watched distractedly.

"Sure you don't want to help?" Emilia asked. She'd finally softened her tone, and Alfie was glad for it.

"I just don't understand Coach," he said for the millionth time.

"The food will taste better if we all pitch in," Emilia said with a smile, and Alfie knew she was trying to help cheer him up.

"Somebody, *pronto!*" Zia said at the stove. "Quick! Get me a pinch of salt!"

Despite his mood, Alfie walked around the counter and took a pinch of salt just like Zia had shown him. He tossed it into the pan as Zia stirred. "There!" she said. "Now it'll really be special."

Chapter 3

For a flash before Alfie and Emilia took their first bite of dinner that night, Alfie thought they were going to be transported again. They'd all helped with dinner, and Zia had that glint in her eyes and kept talking about Naples. As had become their habit, Alfie and Emilia watched each other closely as they took their first bites of any Zia-cooked foods. But aside from their one and only trip to Naples, nothing ever happened. They were starting to think it was some crazy fluke, a strange dream they'd shared.

As it was, Alfie woke up the next morning in his own bed and had to face his own life. A life that involved *not* playing soccer at Saturday's game.

He painfully sat through his classes until the final bell rang and he could go home. That night he was still so mad he could hardly concentrate on the chicken cacciatore Mom and Zia made for dinner. The adults savored every bite, though, and raved as they sat back in their chairs and admired the meal they'd just eaten.

"Maybe next time," Dad said, "you'll let me get in on the cooking. You girls are spoiling me!"

"*Consentono!* We allow you! Just jump in!" Mom said. "You don't have to ask, just start dicing."

"Stepping in between you two in the kitchen can be like stepping in between a matador and a bull," Dad said.

"Where did you find this?" Zia held an asparagus between her fingers like a wand.

"That farmer's market we went to last week," Mom said. "I stopped by on my way to work this morning. I chose just the right ones, don't you think?"

"In Naples you don't have to be an expert—you only have to know your way to the market. The farmers do all the work for you. Remember?" said Zia.

Dad said, "The markets in Naples were a bit crazy, but I loved them. I could buy olives for my mother and a comic book for myself from the same stall."

"The markets where you grow up are always special," Zia said. "But the markets in other places, like Paris, are also hard to beat. The food always takes your breath away."

"Well," Mom said. "The French and their food. They put each meal on a pedestal."

"*Voilà! È fatto così!*" Zia said. "That's how it should be!"

"Hey," Dad said, nudging Alfie with his foot. "Why are you so quiet tonight? Something happen at school?"

"I don't want to talk about it," Alfie mumbled.

Mom pushed herself up from the table and disappeared into the pantry. Calling out to Zia, she said, "I remember how Nona used to make me hot chocolate when I was feeling down."

"Ah, yes!" Zia said. "My sister made the most wonderful hot chocolate in all of Italy. My own grandmother, your great-great-grandmother, had the best recipe," she said to the kids. "So thick and creamy. Hot chocolate is the answer to all of life's little problems. I remember my friend Sonja in Paris was so distraught once that I had to make it for her every night for a week straight. She claims that it was only through my hot chocolate that she was able to cope."

"Who wants a mug?" Mom said.

Zia gasped. "What is that?"

Mom held up a box of hot-chocolate packets and said, "I just said I was going to make it for the kids."

Zia pushed herself up from her chair and said, "Not with that garbage!"

"Zia," Mom began. "Not everything can be made from scratch. If it were up to you, we'd be making our own chocolate."

"Can you do that?" Emilia asked.

"Where do you think chocolate comes from? The chocolate fairy?" Zia's voice called out from the kitchen pantry. Soon she emerged. "Voilà!" In her arms she held chocolate, sugar, and vanilla. "Now, where is that cayenne pepper I saw?" she said, rummaging through the cabinet. "It may not be the French way, but it adds a fun kick to the chocolate."

"Cayenne pepper?" Alfie said. Despite his decision to stay in a bad mood until the week was over, he couldn't help but be curious about Zia's new recipe. He got up from the table to join her in the kitchen. "Come on," he said to his sister. "It's *chocolate*."

Soon the whole family was back in the kitchen with Zia at the helm.

"When I made this for my friend Sonja...," she began. "Ah! Here it is," she said as she spotted the jar of cayenne pepper. "I made enough for both of us—a good friend stays until the last drop."

Emilia smiled as she and Alfie settled themselves into the tall chairs at the island where Zia worked. Mom leaned into Dad in the doorway and watched.

"Your mother is right about one thing," Zia said. "The French take food very seriously. They would never settle for some powdered chocolate nonsense. It's all about quality." She measured out the squares of chocolate as well as the milk. To Emilia she said, "No lazybones—help out. Get me some of that sugar there." Emilia leaned over the counter and measured out the sugar.

"Oh, mademoiselle," Alfie said, pinching his mouth together and going for some sort of French accent. *"Wee, wee, wee! Vwa-lah!"*

Emilia giggled and Dad said, "Bet you can't spell *yes* in French."

"W-E-E!" Alfie spelled, even though he knew he wasn't right.

"Try *O-U-I*," Zia said.

"Nuh-uh," Emilia said. "She's teasing you, Alfie."

"I never joke about French!" Zia said. "It's pronounced *wee* but spelled *O-U-I*. It's all you'll want to say when you're sitting at one of the thousands of little cafés that line the streets and you're looking at a menu full of foods you just want to eat for days. And then you wake up early, and the sun is rising in shades of pink over the white buildings as you make your way through the sleepy streets until you're upon the fresh markets!"

"Like in Naples!" Alfie said. His parents gave him a curious look, so he quickly added, "I mean, like you've said about Naples, right?"

Without missing a beat, Zia said, "There are markets all over the city of Paris. When you live there you find the ones you like the best and shop each morning for the day's foods. My favorite was Rue Marche. It had everything I needed, and I went every morning."

"We like to do big shops," Alfie said. "That way Mom and Dad only have to go to the store once or twice a month."

Zia waved off the comment with a roll of her eyes. "We had the Rue Montorgueil, Rue Mouffetard, Rue Cler for people-watching—I once saw France's first lady there!"

"*Rue, rue, rue,*" Alfie mimicked. "*Oui, oui, oui.*"

"I wish I could go to Paris," Emilia said.

"You would fit right in, *cara ragazza,*" Zia said. "Now, two tiny pinches of the cayenne pepper, and we will almost be ready. One pinch for each of you." She held out the dish of burnt-orange spice. They each tossed a pinch into the bowl.

"Voilà!" Emilia cheered.

As Zia collected mugs she asked Mom and Dad, "You don't want any, do you?"

"No, you go ahead," Dad said. "We're heading upstairs; we've both got some work to do."

"And not too much now," Mom said. "I want you both to clear the table and have your teeth brushed and be in bed in thirty minutes. Understood?"

Zia gave the mixture in the pan a final stir and then carefully poured it into the mugs. Steam rose up and the smell of rich chocolate washed over their faces.

"Maybe if I give Coach some of this, it'll help him calm down and see that I need to be back in the starting lineup," Alfie said. "You think it'll work like that, Zia?" He took a sip and couldn't believe how rich and delicious it was. It was like drinking straight-up melted chocolate. He took another sip. It was warm and thick, like the center of a molten-lava cake. He took another sip, and then another.

"Not in that exact way," she said. "But I think you'll figure this whole thing out. You just need a little perspective. Warmed chocolate can give you that. So what do you think of the hot chocolate, Emilia?"

"*Mmm,*" Emilia said. She took a careful sip and, closing her eyes, said, "Oh . . . my . . . gosh . . ."

Zia smiled at her grand-niece's reaction. "Parisians take their work quite seriously, but they take their enjoyment of the little moments just as seriously. Sometimes sitting in a café with close friends or family and enjoying a shared plate of *macarons* is just as important as sitting in an office working. You know, some Parisians start their morning with a mug of hot chocolate."

"Really?" Emilia asked, taking a fourth and fifth sip.

"The chocolate is like medicine to take away your

troubles and help you see that life is sweet. Go on," she said, gesturing that they should take another sip. "Taste how sweet it is . . ."

Chapter 4

As Alfie took another sip of the sweet, thick chocolate drink, he felt the air shift around him, and an odd feeling welled up in the pit of his stomach. Before he could grab Emilia, he found himself standing on a cobblestoned street. He knew it had happened before, but still—he couldn't believe it! They had been transported again!

"Oh . . . my . . . gosh . . . ," Emilia said. Alfie was glad to know his sister was there, too.

They still held the mugs of hot chocolate in their hands, and Emilia was on the verge of spilling the rest of hers as she spun and looked around.

Alfie, seeing the strange street and bustle of activity,

thought one thing: *Naples!* He'd get to see his friend Marco again!

"What street are we on?" he said, trying to get his bearings. Alfie had an uncanny sense of direction and hoped that if he saw some street names he could find his way back to Trattoria Floreano, the restaurant owned by Marco's family.

"Oh my gosh, oh my gosh, oh my gosh," Emilia continued.

"Calm down," he said. "We need to figure out where we are so we can get to Marco's café." Maybe they could play soccer down by the Gulf of Naples and Marco could give him some pointers.

Alfie figured they had to be in an unfamiliar part of town, because the streets were wider than he remembered. The buildings looked different, too. The buildings he remembered in Naples had been a golden-yellow color with dark orange roofs. These were white with steep black roofs and had wrought-iron balconies.

"Are you blind?" Emilia said. She hopped on her feet like an eager puppy while pointing her finger. "See?"

Alfie followed her finger down the street where he saw, clear as the mug still in his hand, the Eiffel Tower.

"We're in Paris!" Emilia squealed. "Wait till I tell Felicia. She'll die of jealousy!"

"Paris?" Alfie said. He'd been excited to see Marco, and now they were going to have to figure out all over again how to find their way back home. "Great, now what do we do?"

"Aren't you excited?" Emilia said. "Oh my gosh, we have to get croissants and go shopping and eat cheese and walk along the river and—"

"We have to focus," Alfie said. "We can't just hang out here. It doesn't work like that."

"We don't know *how* it works because we still don't know what *it* is," she said. "Zia Donatella is the greatest great-aunt in the entire universe! Can you believe she sent us to *Paris*? Look at that woman's high heels and handbag and sunglasses—she's so chic!" Emilia said of a woman who passed them.

Alfie didn't often pay attention to what his sister said, but he was pretty sure she'd never used the word *chic* before.

They started down the street. Emilia gushed over everything in sight. Alfie expected her to say how beautiful the trash cans were.

"Maybe we should find a café," Alfie said. That was how they met Marco. Maybe it would work again.

"Of course we should go to a café," Emilia said. "Paris is famous for them!"

Alfie spotted a group of kids about their age standing with some adults down the street. Maybe it was a guided tour or something that could help them figure out how to get home.

"Let's go down there," he said. "Maybe we'll meet someone who can help."

Chapter 5

"Let me do the talking," Alfie instructed as they got to the back of the group.

He tapped a boy on the back who rested his knee on a dark blue suitcase. "*Psst,*" he whispered. "Excuse me, um..."

The boy turned and looked at Alfie. He raised a questioning eyebrow.

"Um," Alfie began, "well, this is going to sound really strange, but..." Beside him, Emilia began drifting away from the group toward a nearby shop that sold vintage hats and gloves. Alfie grabbed her wrist and pulled her back, as if she were a balloon floating away.

"You're late," the boy said.

"Late?" Alfie asked.

"You two!" called one of the adults at the front, snapping out each word like a firecracker. The man was short and stout with round glasses and a thin mustache. "Welcome to the Young Chefs School of Fine French Cooking. You're off to a terrible start. You must never be late!"

"Monsieur, please," said the woman next to the angry man—who towered over him. She looked at Alfie and Emilia and said, "Welcome, children. We're happy you've joined us."

"Glad you had time to stop for a drink," the man said, eyeing the Bertolizzis' mugs. "Marcel, check these late arrivals off my list," he said to the younger, skinny guy beside him.

"Name?" Marcel asked, looking down at a clipboard.

Alfie said, "No, you don't under—"

"Emilia and Alfredo Bertolizzi," Emilia said with total confidence.

Marcel searched his clipboard for their names, but of course they weren't listed. He kept flipping the pages back and forth, panic growing in his eyes.

"Ah, Marcel!" the round man said, throwing his hands up in the air. "You're always messing things up! Two missed students, unbelievable. Good thing we have extra beds. Madame Rousseau, can you accommodate these tardy children?"

"Of course," she said, smiling so the corners of her eyes crinkled. "We're very happy to have you."

"Thank you," Emilia said, and Alfie wanted to pull his hair out. What was she doing?

"Now!" the man called. "As I hope you all know, I am Monsieur DuBois, and I run this course along with Madame Rousseau. We have one week to teach you the basics of French cooking, and you will utilize every single lesson, demonstration, and task we teach you. Your parents may think this is a fun camp during your half-term break, but as far as we're concerned you are here to learn, same as at your school."

"We're here to go to school?" Alfie said, but Emilia nudged him quiet.

"Monsieur DuBois," Madame Rousseau said gently. "We are here to have a *little* fun."

"*Humph*," Monsieur DuBois grumbled.

"You can take your bags up to your rooms," Madame Rousseau said. "Since this week is all about food, we begin by going to dinner, so come right back down. We're going to have a great—"

"If you're late, you'll stay here and peel potatoes," Monsieur DuBois said.

Madame Rousseau shook her head. "I'm sure everyone can get back downstairs in ten minutes. Right, students?"

The students grabbed their suitcases and headed inside. Emilia followed.

"Hey, where do you think you're going?" Alfie asked. "We're not staying."

"Then what are we supposed to do?" Emilia said. "Hello? This is a *cooking* school. That means we're going to be surrounded by food and eating the entire time. Food is what got us here and what took us home last time. We *have* to stay."

Alfie thought about his soccer game tomorrow. He didn't want to miss it. When they went to Naples they'd only been there for a day, so he had to think the same thing would happen here in Paris. Right?

"Okay," he said as they followed the others to find their rooms. "But we should definitely stay under the radar. I don't know what'll happen if they find out we're not supposed to be here. Agreed?"

"Yeah, whatever," Emilia said. But Alfie could see in the distracted way she looked toward the stairs that this might not be possible. The last thing they needed was to be asked a bunch of questions that they couldn't answer.

Chapter 6

Alfie entered the room just as the other boys were filing back downstairs for dinner. As several boys pounded down the stairs past Alfie, one stopped just in front of him.

"Come on, you'll be late," he said. It was the boy from outside. He had dark brown skin and light brown eyes. "Trust me—you really don't want Monsieur DuBois yelling at you more than once in a day."

Alfie smiled. He set his mug down. A gigantic orange cat wrapped itself around Alfie's leg. "Where'd the cat come from?"

"That is Lardon, the fattest cat

in Paris and unofficial mascot of the school," he said. "Remember him from the school's brochure?"

They started back down the stairs with Lardon leading the way with heavy paw-steps. "Right," Alfie said.

"Don't leave any food out or he'll eat it," the boy said. "He ate a whole pack of bacon when he was just a kitten. That's how he got his name. I'm Andre, by the way."

"I'm Alfie."

"Where are you from?"

"America," Alfie said. "You from Paris?"

"Yes," Andre said. "Well, I am, but my grandparents are from Gabon, in West Africa. We all live here together."

"Like my family," Alfie said. "My grandparents—and also my parents—they were all born in Italy, but we live in America. So we have something in common."

"The most important things," Andre said. "Family and home."

The students gathered in the lobby to be escorted to dinner. Even though it was a small class, Alfie didn't see his sister. He'd lost her for a time in Naples and couldn't bear for it to happen again. Then he heard a gaggle of kids laughing and clomping down the stairs. He turned to see a group of girls. In the center of them was Emilia—wearing a completely new outfit.

Alfie stepped closer to her and said, "Um, hello? Where'd you get all these clothes? We're supposed to be staying under the radar."

"I am," Emilia said, stepping discreetly away from the girls. "By blending in with everyone. I look good!" She held the ends of the skirt, which had big pleats and a squiggly pattern. "I told them the airline lost our luggage, so Claudette let me borrow this, and Natalie loaned me the top, and then Madeline was like, 'You can't *not* accessorize,' so she loaned me her bracelets. Aren't they pretty?" She jangled a wrist full of metal bracelets in his face.

"Please be—" Just then Andre came and stood near them. "Emilia, this is Andre. Andre, this is my sister, Emilia," Alfie said.

"Hello," they said to each other.

"And this is Madeline," Emilia said, pulling the girl closest to her in for introductions.

"You're Alfredo," she said to Alfie with a smile.

"Hey," he said with a little wave.

"We're both named after foods."

Alfie had no idea what kind of food she was named after, so he just smiled and nodded.

"Okay, students!" Monsieur DuBois said, clapping his hands. "We go to dinner now! Follow me and stay together, please."

Emilia let out an excited squeal. "Dinner! In Paris!"

"Just remember to pay attention to the food," Alfie told her quietly.

"Yes," Andre said, overhearing. "You'll taste flavors you never thought possible. Is this your first time in Paris?"

"Yes," Emilia said.

"Well, then," Andre said, "I think you are in for quite a treat."

Evening was coming on, and the sun began to slip behind the buildings, giving the city a warm glow that made the buildings seem dipped in yellow and pink pastels. Emilia walked ahead of Alfie and Andre with her new friends, talking over each other like they'd all been friends since kindergarten.

The restaurant was not like the chain restaurants the Bertolizzis were used to visiting. Sure, since Zia came to town they'd been eating lots more meals at home. But before all that, if they didn't order pizza they might go out to Wallobee's or Manny's House of Yum, where the waiters made you wear balloon hats and shook noisemakers at your ears if anyone suspected it was your birthday.

This restaurant didn't even have a television in it. It had white tablecloths and the waiters—mostly older gentlemen with white hair—wore white shirts with black vests and long black aprons that reached their ankles.

The class sat at a long table filled with more silverware than Alfie had ever seen. As menus were passed out, the class went around the table and introduced themselves. Emilia, who sat next to Alfie, enthusiastically said her name and that she was just *so happy* to be here in the City of Light.

City of Light? Please! Alfie kicked her under the table, but she ignored him.

Alfie's and Emilia's eyes ran down the menu. They had no idea how to begin or what to order. When the waiter came around, Alfie simply pointed without any idea of what it was. Emilia ordered the same as Madeline, who sat on her other side.

Monsieur DuBois ordered several appetizers for the table. When they arrived Alfie and Emilia followed everyone's lead and picked up a tiny fork and speared something that looked like a chicken wing.

"Tell me, class," Monsieur DuBois began, "what flavors do you taste in this?"

Alfie tasted the meat. It flaked like fish but tasted like chicken. He liked it, but the other kids started talking about all the tiny little subtle flavors they tasted. Madeline said lemon. Andre tasted garlic. A boy named Jacques said there was a hint of parsley.

"Very good, students," Madame Rousseau said. "Excellent palates!"

"It's really good, huh?" Emilia said, chomping through her last bite. "You gonna eat that?" She pointed to the other half of Alfie's appetizer. He wanted to finish it, but his sister obviously liked it, so he decided to be nice and let her have it. Besides, there were plenty more appetizers on the table to taste. He helped himself to a little fried potato chunk and took a bite. It tasted buttery and creamy.

Emilia bit into the appetizer she had snatched from Alfie's plate. "Yum!" she said, and Alfie couldn't help but laugh at his sister's enthusiasm.

"They're good, right?" Madeline asked Emilia.

"I love them," Emilia said. "Alfie, we gotta make these back home."

"For sure," Alfie answered, scooping up some gooey cheese with a few crusts of bread. He slathered the cheese on the bread and said through a full mouth, "They don't taste like any chicken wings we've ever had."

"Chicken wings?" Madeline said. "They're frog legs."

Emilia immediately began spitting out the last bits of food into her cloth napkin.

"Are you joking?"

Madeline stifled a smile. "No, they are."

"Emilia, you said you liked them," Alfie reminded her. He scooped another bite of the cheese and bread—it was warm and oozed slightly over the edge of the bread. He added a slather of purple olive spread, which gave each bite a tangy flavor.

"You knew and let me finish yours," she said.

"I didn't know." He laughed.

"Alfie!"

"Hey," the boy named Jacques said. "Who ate all the Brie?"

"And the olive spread is more than half gone," said Dillon, a boy with neatly trimmed hair and a shirt and tie.

Alfie looked down at his plate. The Brie must have been the ooey-gooey cheese he'd had three tastes of with that soft, crusty bread, topped with two scoopfuls of the olive spread.

Jacques saw the leftover evidence on Alfie's plate and said, "It's for all of us. We're supposed to share."

"Oops, sorry," Alfie said. But how was he supposed to help himself with all this amazing food?

The rest of the dinner was full of more great food, presented on gleaming white plates and artfully arranged with meats, sides, and sauces that resembled small paintings. Alfie had chosen—or pointed to—a beef dish with a burgundy-colored sauce that was slightly sweet and incredibly rich. Emilia and Madeline had a roasted chicken that looked nothing like the ones their mom sometimes picked up in the heated display in the grocery store.

By the time they got back to the school, Alfie's mind was as full with the day's adventures as his belly was with food. But now they'd been here almost a full day, just like in Naples. That time they'd made their way back before it was time for bed, so already Alfie was confused. They didn't know how this whole thing worked, but they couldn't stay overnight. Surely something would happen at any moment that would take them home.

Chapter 7

Alfie opened his eyes. The room was dark and cold. As he sat up in bed, he knew where he was but still crept to the window to double-check. Five stories below him was a Paris street, cobblestoned and curved slightly at the base of the building. He was going to miss his soccer game. But if he was only going to sit on the bench, what did it matter? The bigger problem was what his mom and dad would do when they realized he and Emilia had disappeared. Zia would have to confess that she'd worked some crazy magic into those mugs of hot chocolate. Alfie took in a deep breath and something wonderful filled his nose—the scent of freshly baked bread. He immediately thought of the homemade pizza dough he'd learned to make in Naples. Alfie decided to take this as a sign to try and stay positive. Another comforting sign was Lardon, rubbing his soft fur on Alfie's leg. Alfie reached down to pet his head, which Lardon only allowed for a moment. The cat soon turned away and headed out of the room.

The other boys were just waking up and everyone walked sleepily to the bathrooms to brush their teeth and wash their faces.

"Breakfast is in the café downstairs," Andre said to Alfie with a yawn. "Then class is in the kitchen."

All Alfie could do was get dressed in yesterday's clothes and hope no one noticed—except they did.

"Isn't that the same shirt you wore yesterday?" Andre asked.

"Um, yeah," Alfie said. Remembering Emilia's fib, he said, "The airline lost our luggage. But I'm pretty sure we'll get it back today." He hoped they wouldn't be here more than two days. They definitely couldn't stay all week—Alfie couldn't even begin to think about that.

He followed Andre and Jacques downstairs and directly next door to the café, where the smell of fresh bread engulfed Alfie's senses. The café was full of customers, and not just from the Young Chefs School.

Activity filled the small space where people sat at round tables, sipping from steaming mugs that were topped with swirls of white from warm milk. Alfie searched for Emilia and spotted her at a table in the corner with Madeline, Claudette, and Natalie.

"I'll grab us a table," Andre said.

"We can just go to the counter to order," said Jacques, who was dressed for the day in a green button-down, which strained over his round belly. Alfie followed him but kept an eye on Emilia. "Everything is very good. Of course Paris pastries are legendary, so you have to try one: brioche, apple turnover, cinnamon roll, and the king of all pastries, the croissant. Mother calls them empty calories, but I  call them"—he patted his round belly—"part of my job as an aspiring chef. Then you get your drink—coffee or hot chocolate. Have you ever had a café au lait?"

Alfie was overwhelmed at the sight of all the pastries, but when Jacques said *hot chocolate*, Alfie focused.

"Sorry, Jacques," Alfie said. "I was going to eat breakfast with my sister."

Jacques looked over Alfie's shoulder at Emilia sitting with the girls. "Really?"

"She forgot, I guess," Alfie said. "Wait for me afterward and we'll go to class together, okay?"

"Sure, okay," he said. "I'll tell Andre."

Alfie took his sister by the arm and pulled her aside. "We're still here!" he hissed. "Zia is going to have to explain everything to Mom and Dad. Even if they believe her, they are going to freak out. I'm hoping hot chocolate will get us back. We need to get some for breakfast— now!"

"I don't know why you're obsessed with going home," Emilia complained as Alfie pulled her away from the table.

"Uh, because it's where we live?" he said. "And I'm

not obsessed—I'm just trying to be responsible. Plus, we stayed overnight. That's huge and kind of scary, don't you think?"

"I guess," Emilia said. "Okay, I'll try, but only because I was going to have it for breakfast anyway."

At the counter he held up two fingers and pointed to the chocolate croissants behind the glass case and asked for two hot chocolates as well. The man behind the counter nodded and prepared their order. Since they were part of the cooking school, their meals were supposed to be included in their tuition—even though Alfie and Emilia weren't actually enrolled.

They found a table way in the back. Alfie insisted on thinking of a memory together and then taking a sip at the same time.

Alfie said, "Remember how Zia got so mad when Mom brought out the powdered hot chocolate? It was like she'd totally offended Zia."

Emilia cracked a small smile. "I had no idea Zia had a

stash of good chocolate in the pantry. I'm going to look for the rest of it when we get home."

They both took a sip of their hot chocolate.

It was beyond rich, maybe even richer than Zia Donatella's. It was like drinking a cake, and they couldn't get enough. This hot chocolate didn't have that tiny bit of heat that Zia's had, but it was still velvety and yummy and tasted like total heaven. Also, it was completely not working.

"Try again," Alfie insisted.

Emilia was already taking another sip. With a chocolate mustache she said, "It's not working, but maybe we should just keep drinking until it does." Alfie noticed that the other students dunked their croissants into their hot chocolate.

"Let's try dunking," Alfie said.

"Hurry up, then, I'm starving," Emilia said.

They dunked their croissants and took big bites, but nothing happened.

"Time for class!" Andre called out to Alfie and Emilia from across the café. The other students were quickly finishing up breakfast.

"I could sit and sip this all day," Emilia said, cramming the croissant into her mouth and slurping the hot chocolate. "Come on," she said, standing up. "We don't want to be late."

Alfie walked out of the café to face whatever was coming next. One thing was sure—drinking the same thing that had brought them to Paris wasn't working. He and Emilia would have to figure out just what it was that would take them back.

Chapter 8

When they got to the kitchen, the students were given chef's jackets, pants, and hats that they were to wear anytime they were in the kitchen or out on a school assignment. Alfie felt very official in his tall white hat, while Emilia posed like she was wearing some fancy Parisian fashions.

"Stand up straight, now. Line up. Come on!" Monsieur DuBois clapped his hands to get the students to simmer down after their excitement over the uniforms. Everyone scrambled into position, as if they were getting ready for a military inspection, with Alfie and Emilia directly in the middle.

"Now!" Monsieur DuBois continued. "Every moment in Paris is a chance to learn about our culinary history. Everything goes back to food. So that is what our next exercise is all about. Madame Rousseau! Tell the children!"

Madame Rousseau gave Monsieur DuBois a weary look. Then she turned to the class, a smile spreading across her face. "We have something very special planned," she began. "I would call it less an exercise and more of a ... scavenger hunt!"

The class began to cheer.

"So," Madame Rousseau said. "There will be two teams. Each will get three clues. This is all about the food of Paris, and it's meant to be fun, but—"

"But it is also a lesson of the food we have here in our fine city," Monsieur DuBois said. "Do not eat the food you collect, as you will need to bring it all back here for a lesson."

"Yes," Madame Rousseau said. "A lesson as well as a feast, so make sure you study the clues in order to get the correct foods. We'll split into groups. Emilia and everyone to her right, you'll go with Monsieur DuBois," she said, touching Emilia's head. "Alfie and those to his left, you'll come with me," she continued. He and Emilia were being split into separate teams, and Alfie saw panic in her eyes.

"It'll be okay," he told her.

"But I'm stuck with Monsieur DuBois!" she whispered, and Alfie suddenly realized she didn't mind being separated from *him*.

"Let's break into groups and go over our first clues, because *time starts now!*" Madame Rousseau cheered.

A mad scramble started to get into groups and grab hold of the first clue.

"Who wants to be in charge of the map?"

In that quick moment, Alfie forgot all about Emilia.

"I do!" he said, taking the map held out by Madame Rousseau.

The team gathered around: Alfie, Madeline, Jacques, and Andre.

"Okay, everyone, here we go," said Jacques. He read the first clue out loud: "'At the top of the hill is a sacred white dome; not far away is a taste of home. With ingredients so simple it could be made by a beginner; go where the four ingredients are made and taste the real winner.'"

"The top of Paris—the Eiffel Tower?" Alfie suggested.

"No," said Jacques. "The top of the hill—that's got to be

Sacré-Coeur, don't you think?"

"Yes!" Madeline agreed. "The dome. And 'ingredients so simple' . . . what is made near there?"

"What kinds of food carts are near Sacré-Coeur?" Andre asked.

Taste the real winner reminded Alfie of Naples and the big pizza-making contest. He'd watched the Floreano family make their own pizza dough with just a few ingredients: flour, yeast, salt, and water—four ingredients! "Hey," he said. "Are they making, like, pizza dough or something? I was in Naples once and there was this pizza-making contest . . ."

"Perhaps something a bit more French?" Madame Rousseau said.

"Baguettes!" Andre exclaimed.

Madeline clapped her hands. "That's it! The baguette competition! Who won this year?" She looked at Jacques.

After a beat he said, "Boulangerie Marchal. In Montmartre, which is—"

"Near Sacré-Coeur!" Andre said. "We'll take the *métro*. I think there's a station near here."

Alfie studied the map as they raced out of the school. He quickly found the station and traced his finger up to Sacré-Coeur, leaving Emilia's team behind.

Along with Madame Rousseau, the team headed toward the Paris *métro* station, with Alfie calling out directions even though Jacques seemed to know where to go. They easily spotted the red *métro* sign with the fancy letters and dashed down the stairs.

Alfie had never ridden a subway before—he felt like he was going on a ride at an amusement park. Madame Rousseau had tickets prepared and handed one to each student.

When they emerged from the subway, Alfie's eyes landed on a huge white basilica with three domes and several turret-like spires around it.

"It's this way," Jacques said. "My dad and I have been here dozens of times."

From down the street they spotted the bakery, jutting to a point where two merging streets met, the paneling painted a rustic blue. Despite the long line, they squeezed into the tiny shop. Madeline held up the clue and said to the boy behind the counter, "We found you!"

He grinned, obviously knowing the game, and went to get the team's second clue while Alfie let his eyes and nose become overwhelmed by the smell of the fresh bread and the rows upon rows of baguettes. When the boy came back, he gave Madeline the next clue as well as three baguettes, which Madame Rousseau paid for.

The team raced outside to read their next clue. They gathered around Madeline as she read: "'In pinks, lilacs, yellows, and greens; this is a treat that tastes simply supreme; a delicate crunch on the outside and soft on the in; it's not a baguette you crave but a sweet for the end.'"

"It's dessert!" Jacques said. "I always know when it's time for dessert. And the colors—it's so obvious!"

"*Macarons*," Andre and Madeline said together.

Alfie didn't know what those were, but he thought he remembered Zia mentioning them. Madeline read on: "'Go to the place they were invented, where their taste is still the most splendid; it's on Paris's most famous street, next to the park where people meet.'"

"Okay, where is that?" Alfie said, stretching out his map.

"Champs-Élysées, obviously. We have to get back on the *métro*," Andre said. "If we head down this way, we'll be one stop closer. But we have to run!"

"No running!" Madame Rousseau said. "It's too much for me, and I don't want you all to get hurt."

Still, they walked quickly as Alfie consulted the map carefully. "Looks like we should transfer to the one line and get off at—hey! Franklin D. Roosevelt. That's our stop.

You know, he's an American—"

"No, we should get off at George V," Jacques said. "Trust me, it's closer."

"Okay, sure," Alfie said as he folded up his map, feeling defeated.

"Don't worry," Madeline said, pulling him along. "It's just because we're from here."

"Everyone here grew up in Paris?" Alfie asked.

"Most of us," she said. "My family moved here when I was just five, so really, it's all I remember. My parents have their own catering business, so I know a little about food, too."

"Probably more than a little," Alfie said.

"Probably." She smiled. "I want to work with them one day. They already let me do little things to help out. They say you can never stop learning, which is why they sent me here to the school. Isn't that why you're here—to learn about French food?"

"Yeah," Alfie said. "Of course."

When they arrived at their next stop they were on a wide street called Champs-Élysées, which was lined with trees and posh stores. Everyone seemed a little more elegantly dressed—except the tourists, who Alfie easily spotted by their comfortable shoes and baseball caps.

At the shop of their next clue, Alfie saw a window display full of pastel circles the size of Oreo cookies, but definitely fancier. They looked so pretty he could hardly believe they could eat them.

Inside, the walls and ceiling were golden with honey-colored light and small dangling chandeliers. Emilia would go crazy in here!

Madeline got the attention of a lady behind the counter, who took out an empty box and said, "No clue until the box is full." She gestured to the display case filled with rainbows of colors and flavors.

"Fine by us!" Jacques said. "I could fill ten boxes and it still wouldn't be enough. Oh, *macarons*, how I love you so!" he said, and everyone laughed.

Alfie learned that *macarons* were sweet treats made from meringue and basic stuff like powdered and granulated sugar, egg whites, and ground almonds and sandwiched around a thin layer of buttercream or jam.

They chose a beautiful variety of flavors—almond,

hazelnut, pistachio, raspberry, and strawberry, as well as strange flavors (to Alfie) like violet, rose, black currant, and caramel with salted butter.

Before he could take in the rainbow of *macarons*, their next and final clue took them to a cheese shop.

To get to Fromagerie Barthélémy, the team crossed back over the River Seine and past Les Invalides, a cluster of museums and monuments. The cheese monger's shop was in a tiny space along a quaint side street. He proudly showed the team his huge selection of French cheeses. Some were hard, some soft, some smelled lightly fragrant, some smelled so much like rotten dirty feet that it made Alfie want to gag. If any of them tasted like that Brie cheese he had last night, though, he'd eat it no matter what it smelled like.

Bart, the owner of the shop, took them to the cave downstairs where the cheese was ripened. Down a narrow, curving staircase, they entered a room with a low brick ceiling and saw giant disks of cheese as big as car tires lined up on wooden tables and shelves. This was completely different from the *mozzarella di bufala* that Alfie saw made in Naples.

The students chose a mild, soft cheese called Camembert, then started back to the school. They'd circled the whole city and were able to walk back, with Jacques leading the way and Alfie paying attention to each street corner and fountain they passed.

Finally they were back in the kitchen, which they found empty. They were the first ones back!

"Can we start eating?" asked Jacques.

"Wait patiently for the others," Madame Rousseau said.

When the others arrived half an hour later, they did not look happy.

"What happened?" Alfie asked Emilia.

"Monsieur DuBois made everything into a *lesson*," she said. "And you know it's bad when *I'm* bored by a lesson—especially about Paris. He went on and on about the birth of the Paris cafés until we were falling asleep over our café au laits."

"You had coffee?"

"It was decaf, but, yeah. It was okay. I'd rather have had more hot chocolate."

"What foods did you get?"

"Wait till you see!" she said, finally smiling.

Madame Rousseau called everyone to attention.

"Very good, everyone," she said. "I hope the trip gave you a nice view of Paris and its wonderful food. Now—is anyone hungry?"

Chapter 9

The students dove into the pile of food at the center of the prep table. Jacques and Madeline went for the *macarons*, Emilia snagged some chocolate, and Alfie ripped off a piece of bread and grabbed a knife to spread some cheese. They were like savages who hadn't eaten in a month.

"Slow down!" Monsieur DuBois called. "We have lessons for each of the foods. For example, the *macaron* was invented here in France. Do not listen to people who try to tell you it comes from England or Italy! We French know better." He paused for a moment. "Is anyone listening?"

Madame Rousseau said, "Students, if you want to keep eating, you must listen."

The students quieted down. Eating quietly while
pretending to listen to a lecture on the history of French
cheese making, the invention of the *macaron*, and more
was better than not eating at all.

Once the food was gone and Monsieur DuBois had talked himself hoarse, Madame Rousseau told the students about the next part of cooking camp.

"The teams you were in for the scavenger hunt are your teams for the next challenge," Madame Rousseau said. "You will each prepare a meal for us and a guest. The winning team gets—"

"Not just any guest," Monsieur DuBois interrupted. "An extraordinary guest, a *great* guest! Chef Auguste Orleans, a national treasure and my own former instructor, will dine with us. Students, it is extremely important that you take this seriously."

"Well, yes," Madame Rousseau said, eyeing Monsieur DuBois. "Try your hardest, as we know you will. But we know that you don't have all the experience of an *adult chef.*"

"They can still try," Monsieur DuBois said.

Madame Rousseau sighed. "As I was saying, we have a most excellent prize for the winner—dinner at Le Jules Verne restaurant atop the Eiffel Tower."

Everyone got excited at this announcement, but Emilia was jumping up and down and clapping her hands as if she'd already won.

"I'll take that to mean you're excited about this," Madame Rousseau said. "Now it's time to choose your team leader, so gather around and vote."

Alfie wanted to be the leader, even though he felt slightly out of his league after that scavenger hunt.

"So, any volunteers?" Madeline asked. Everyone eyed one another. No one wanted to speak up first.

"Do you want to be captain, Jacques?" Madeline asked.

"I guess I could," Jacques said.

"Or maybe Madeline," Andre said. "You were really good on the scavenger hunt."

"Thanks," she said. "Yeah, if you want, I could be captain."

"But if you don't want to be," Andre quickly said. "I can be."

"Like I said," Jacques said, stepping in. "I don't mind being the team captain."

Alfie saw a great opportunity to settle this once and for all. "I'll be captain. Back home I'm practically the captain of my soccer team, so I have a lot of experience in, you know, leadership and stuff."

The others turned to look at him. "But you didn't even know what a *macaron* was," Jacques said plainly.

"Yeah, but it's about leadership, not cookies," Alfie said.

"*Macarons* aren't cookies." Madeline laughed.

"I *have* been around food—you know, because of my father—since I was a baby. I'll take the nomination," Jacques said.

"We've all been around food since we were babies," Alfie muttered.

"I guess Jacques is a good option," Andre said, looking resigned.

"Yeah, I guess," Madeline said. "That okay, Alfie?"

They could have at least pretended to consider him, but he went ahead and agreed to elect Jacques as team captain.

They headed upstairs to the boys' room, away from the other team, to plan their winning menu.

"You have more experience," Andre said to Jacques as they discussed who should do the main dish.

"Plus," Madeline said, "you can't deny that being taught by one of the best chefs in all of France is a great advantage."

"It doesn't mean I'm any better than anyone," Jacques said sternly. "Besides, we have to work together. This is a competition—we have to win."

"Agreed," Alfie said. Finally something he could understand!

"I think we should do a fancy meal service," Andre said. "Really show off."

"I think we should do simple, classic cooking," Madeline said.

"Alfie, what do you think?" Jacques asked.

"Whatever will help us win." He still felt a bit sour about the whole captain thing.

"But what's your *opinion*?" Jacques pressed. "You have to help us."

"I am helping," Alfie said.

"I mean by having an opinion," Jacques said. "What's the one dish you're really good at making?"

Three sets of eyes stared at Alfie, waiting for him to answer. Although Zia Donatella and his mom had been cooking a lot more at home and he was tasting better and more interesting foods, he still didn't really know how to cook anything on his own.

"Well, I can make pasta," he offered. Zia had taught him how to know when it was perfectly *al dente*—although he still didn't know how to make sauce.

"You can make pasta from scratch?" Madeline said, impressed.

"Well, I mean . . . ," he began. What he'd meant was, he could dump a box into boiling water and know when it was perfectly *al dente*. Sort of.

"We need to do *French* cooking," Jacques said.

"How about if I make a classic French vegetable soup for a starter?" Madeline offered. "That's simple, but it lets the ingredients shine. I heard Monsieur DuBois say we're going to the market tomorrow to get our ingredients, so I'll pick the freshest and best."

"Great start," Jacques said, writing it down. "Andre? Any ideas?"

"My grandmother taught me how to make her famous sausage wrapped in pastry. It was the first thing she learned to make when she moved here from Gabon. I can't do it as well as she can, but it'll make a good first course."

"Sounds excellent," Jacques said, adding it to the list. "I guess my dad did teach me to do steak really well. If I can find a great cut at the market I'll do it *au poivre*. Sound okay?"

Feeling silly, Alfie raised his hand and said, "What's *au poivre*?"

Madeline said, "You know—'with pepper.'"

"Oh, yeah," Alfie replied, hoping he sounded convincing.

"Now all we need is dessert," Jacques said. "Looks like it's you, Alfie. Are you okay with that?"

"Yeah, totally," he said, even though the only dessert he'd made on his own was putting prepared cookie dough discs on a pan and shoving them into the oven.

"Any ideas?" Jacques asked. Alfie stared blankly, his mind racing for something, anything, besides ice cream with store-bought chocolate sauce.

"Jacques, your dad has that awesome raspberry charlotte recipe," Andre said. "That'd be a great finish to our meal."

"Doesn't that recipe take a long time?" Madeline asked.

"Yeah, sort of," Jacques agreed. "There are a lot of steps, but if you pay close attention it's doable. I don't know—maybe there's an easier version that Alfie could do."

"Yeah," Madeline agreed. "Something simple that can't be messed up."

"Hey," Alfie said, insulted. "I can handle it." Maybe he didn't have all their training—or even know what a "raspberry charlotte" was—but he could certainly follow a recipe.

"Are you sure?" Jacques asked, annoying Alfie further.

"I'm sure," he said. "Just give me the recipe, and I'll make the best raspberry dessert you've ever had."

"Charlotte," Jacques said. "Raspberry *charlotte*."

"Whatever."

"Okay, I guess. I'll get you the recipe," Jacques said. He looked down at his list and said, "Well, I guess that's it. We have our menu."

"Good job, everyone," Madeline said.

"So, tomorrow morning we're all going to the markets to gather ingredients," Jacques said. "Then tomorrow afternoon, we'll start our prep, and on Friday we finish and present our meals."

"Sounds like a plan," Alfie said with all the confidence he could muster. But the truth was, he had a really bad feeling that he could be the one to lose this for everyone.

Chapter 10

"All this talk about food has made me hungry," Jacques said. "Want to go to a café?"

"I'm going to meet up with the girls," Madeline said. "I heard they're going to Notre Dame."

"Have fun," Andre said.

Jacques led Alfie and Andre out of the school and down the street, taking corners and turns like he'd done it a million times—which he probably had. They came upon a café with red awnings hanging above small round tables with wire-backed chairs. Jacques chose a table outside. Even though it was a little bit chilly, they had a great view of the bustling crowd on the sidewalks and a large

spraying fountain across the street.

"Café Bertrand is one of my favorite cafés," Jacques

said. "Any time I have extra money I come here for an

omelet at lunch."

"Eggs for lunch?" Alfie asked.

"Of course, why not?" Jacques asked. The waiter came over for their order. Alfie ordered the same as Jacques. "Have you been here before?" Jacques asked Andre.

"No, but there's a place my grandmother takes me not too far from here on St-Germain-des-Prés," Andre said. "They have really good fries that I like to get. My grandmother is the one who taught me to cook."

"Who taught you to cook?" Jacques asked Alfie.

"My *zia*. That means *aunt* in Italian," he said. "She's actually my great-aunt, but we just call her Zia. She's traveled the world, and now she's staying with us for a while. She and my mom cook together, and Emilia and I help out sometimes."

The waiter came by and dropped off their food. The omelet was neatly rolled and a perfectly golden yellow. Alfie cut off a bite.

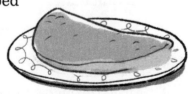

"So then your mom cooks, too," Andre said, biting into his ham-and-cheese sandwich, which was golden and crispy with cheese oozing out the sides.

"No. Well, yes. Sometimes," he said. He chewed his omelet and couldn't believe how good it tasted. The eggs were warm and fluffy, and the cheese and chives were creamy but not too overpowering. "What kind of cheese is this?" It was yet another kind of cheese, different from the one on the first night and the cheese they got on the scavenger hunt. *How many different kinds of cheese do they make in this country?* he wondered.

"Gruyère," Jacques said. "It's good, isn't it?"

Alfie shoveled in another bite. "So good!" he said through a mouthful while Jacques and Andre laughed.

"He has an appetite like me," Jacques said, tucking into another bite.

"Mom used to cook with Zia when she was younger, and now that Zia is staying with us she's started again," Alfie said through a mouthful. He took another bite of the creamy, fluffy omelet. "Last Saturday they made breakfast for us. Not an omelet—the eggs were scrambled with shredded cheese sprinkled in." He took another bite. "We were all in our pajamas, and Dad had just turned on the heat for the first time all season. Emilia was wrapped in a blanket. Mom made the bacon, but Zia made the eggs, and we all argued over what movie we would watch at home while Mom begged Dad to start a fire in the fireplace. It was a great day." He took another bite and closed his eyes, letting the hearty yet delicate dish warm him up.

Suddenly, Alfie felt like he was spinning. He felt his stomach drop. It was happening—he was leaving Paris in the middle of this café in front of his new friends . . . and without his sister.

Chapter 11

Alfie spit the eggs out onto the table.

"Hey, watch it!"

"Gross! What's wrong with you?"

"Sorry," Alfie stammered. He had to get to his sister. He had to tell her that he almost left Paris. At least, he thought that's what just happened. And what if—what if she was somewhere, eating something and leaving without him? They never should have separated.

"I need to find my sister," Alfie said.

"Isn't she with the girls at Notre Dame?" Andre said.

"Can you take me there?"

Jacques and Andre both nodded. "Of course," Jacques

said. "We'll go right now. I know the way."

Andre signaled for the waiter, and Jacques scooped up the last bits of his own omelet as they stood to go. "Sorry," he said through a mouthful. "It's just so good."

Alfie looked at his own half-eaten omelet. He also wanted to finish it, but he couldn't risk going back home without his sister.

After paying for their meal, the boys led Alfie through the streets, and Alfie tried to pay attention so that he could find his way back on his own if he had to. Alfie was good with directions, but he hoped he could remember it all in his worried state.

He saw the French gothic beauty of Notre Dame before they even crossed the bridge over the River Seine—two huge towers rising above

circular windows and three arched doorways at its base. As he got closer, he spotted its famed gargoyles watching the crowd from high above.

"There they are," Andre said, pointing to a bench where the girls sat. But Alfie didn't see Emilia.

They raced over.

"Hey," Jacques said. "How is the planning going?"

"Trying to steal our secrets?" Claudette teased.

"Alfie's looking for his sister," Andre said.

"She's inside," Madeline said. To Alfie she said, "She's completely obsessed. She loves this building. I mean, who wouldn't, but it's like she could just about move in here. Want me to take you inside to get her?"

"That's okay," Alfie said. "Thanks."

He walked through the crowd of tourists toward the entrance, feeling the power of the giant wooden doors and the row of life-size statues of kings above him. Inside, the ceiling rose up several stories high, peaked in the center. In front of him was a gorgeous, colorful series of stained glass that stretched the width of the interior.

As he walked quietly through the cathedral, he couldn't help but think of the church in Naples where Emilia had gone when they were separated. She loved history so much it was no wonder she was somewhere in here, soaking it all in.

He found her near the front standing below a statue of a girl dressed in armor. Alfie let out a sigh of relief—at least he hadn't lost her.

"Who is that?" Alfie asked, standing next to his sister.

She looked over at him. "Hey." Looking back at the statue she said, "Joan of Arc. She didn't make it into the cathedral until 1909. Guess how old this place is?"

"Emilia, we have to talk."

"They started building it in 1163. Can you believe that? And it took almost one hundred and eighty years to finish.

Bet you don't know what *Notre Dame* means."

"Something's happened. It's serious."

"'Our Lady,'" Emilia said. "Makes sense, right?"

"I was eating earlier and I almost went back."

Finally, Emilia turned to face him. "Really?"

"Yes, really," Alfie said. "I was at this café with Andre and Jacques eating an omelet and telling them about that morning at home when we were all eating breakfast together in our pajamas. I closed my eyes and, well"—he shrugged—"I started to get that ... feeling. And then I panicked and spit out the food. I guess it stopped me from going back."

"Jacques and Andre must have thought that was totally normal," she said sarcastically.

"Yeah, they were only slightly suspicious," Alfie joked. "I told them I had to find you. I didn't really give an explanation. Emilia, the café is on the way back. We both have to order that omelet."

"But the banquet is coming up," she said. "Can't we just stay for that? Especially if you figured out the way back."

"Emilia, we can't stay here forever."

"I'm not saying forever," she said. "But dinner at the top of the Eiffel Tower . . . Alfie, please. It's just a little longer."

When he looked at his sister, with her pleading face, standing in this gothic cathedral full of the kind of history she loved, he reconsidered. He may have already missed the soccer game and he did find the way back—he was pretty sure that omelet at that café was the way back. When he looked at her pleading eyes, begging him to stay—how could he say no?

So he decided to stay. Where was the harm in that?

Chapter 12

Just like the day before, Alfie woke up in Paris. Part of him felt scared about being here for so long, over several nights even; a bigger part of him felt ready to take on the day—and the competition.

The boys dressed in their black-and-white–checked chef's pants and pulled on their jackets. Beneath the jacket Alfie wore the same shirt he was wearing the day he arrived.

"Still no luggage?" Jacques asked as Alfie buttoned up the jacket.

"No," Alfie said, not looking him in the eye. "Guess not."

"You should probably tell Madame Rousseau," Jacques said. "Maybe she can call the airline or something."

"Yeah," agreed Andre. "It's strange that nothing has shown up after two days."

After another crazy-yummy breakfast at the café next door, the students put on their chef's hats and headed out for one of the many markets just a few blocks away. Despite the fact that it was ridiculously early, Emilia bounced along with her girlfriends, laughing and talking. She was dressed once again in a put-together outfit no doubt loaned from each of the three girls. If they stayed much longer, she'd probably start wearing a beret.

The Rue Poncelet market was near the Arc de Triomphe. This market was dedicated to rows of lush, colorful vegetables and fruits—everything was so shiny and colorful that Alfie couldn't believe it was real. Artichokes, radishes, and figs—items he'd heard of but never tasted—and fresh herbs like parsley and dill that he'd only ever seen in jars in his mom's spice cabinet were all neatly lined up in the stalls along the street. The market was a couple of streets long. It was more organized than the one in Naples, but the food was just as beautiful. Parisians browsed the selections and the stores behind the stalls for the best ingredients of the day.

The instructors had given each student a small allowance to buy ingredients for the upcoming dinner competition, and it was up to the students to properly budget their money.

Alfie, Jacques, Andre, and Madeline eyed the foods they passed, picking up different pieces of produce to find the perfect freshness.

Alfie eyed Emilia and her team, who were laughing and pointing at a display of some very strange-looking fish.

"Everything all right?" Monsieur DuBois asked, suddenly by Alfie's side.

Seeing the instructor, Alfie's teammates scampered away. *Traitors*, he thought, *leaving me alone with DuBois.*

"Yes," Alfie said. "Just checking things out."

"You know, when I think back to the day you arrived,"
he said, "I don't remember seeing you or your sister
carrying any luggage. You do have luggage, correct?"

Alfie realized he'd have to repeat Emilia's fib to cover his tracks. "The airline lost our luggage, but I'm sure they'll deliver it . . . soon."

"Tell Madame Rousseau," Monsieur DuBois said. "She'll get you and your sister toothbrushes and such until it arrives. I hope you're enjoying our school. Learning lots?"

"Yes," Alfie said, nervous under the chef's scrutiny.

"How did you and your sister learn about the school all the way in the States?"

"Um, through the Internet," Alfie said, picking up a bunch of carrots and then putting it back. Where were fresh raspberries when you needed them to escape from your crazy instructor?

"I only ask," Monsieur DuBois continued, "because we never did find your names on our registration list. Perhaps you should give us your parents' phone number so that we have it on file like we do for the other students."

"Okay," Alfie said. "It's just that, I'm not sure they can be reached right now, is all."

"Still, Madame Rousseau and I will feel better having that number. And since the airline lost your luggage, I want your parents to know that you are being cared for."

Alfie finally came upon a stall selling raspberries. He took the first basketful he saw and quickly paid for it. "I have everything we need. Can we go back to my team?"

Monsieur DuBois looked at him carefully. "Yes, I suppose. Just don't forget about that phone number. Understood?"

"Yes, sir," Alfie said.

As they all walked back to the school, Alfie knew he had two options: stay in Paris and try to win the competition but run the risk of being found out by Monsieur DuBois, or take Emilia straight to the café and get themselves home.

He knew what he had to do.

Chapter 13

Alfie just couldn't help himself. He had to win.

It may have been a petty thing, but when a competition was put before him he had to win it—even if he wasn't sure he actually *could* do that something, which in this case was make a raspberry charlotte. Plus, he told himself, he wanted to do something nice for Emilia. She wanted to stay here in Paris so badly. Who was he to deny her the great experience of being in one of the world's most sophisticated cities?

Once they were all back in the kitchen, Madame Rousseau began the day's lesson. She demonstrated how to make crepes, which were kind of like really thin pancakes. They were also sort of like burritos, because you could fill them with stuff—anything from ham, eggs, and cheese to chocolate hazelnut spread—then roll them up.

Once Madame Rousseau showed everyone how to swirl the batter around in the pan and the hard part of flipping it over, each student got a chance to make one. They even got to choose which items to fill their crepes with. Everyone laughed as they tried flipping the crepe over—Emilia's hit the side of the pan and slid down onto her foot, and Andre flipped his so high it almost touched the ceiling. Alfie concentrated on his flip and did it perfectly on the first try, letting out an intense little "YES!" He filled his crepe with bananas and chocolate sauce and whipped cream that did not come from a squirt can.

Finally, the students were allowed to begin the preparations for their dinners. They broke into their teams, separating on either side of the kitchen.

"Okay!" Jacques began. "Let's get started. Alfie, you sure you're okay with the cake?"

"Yeah, I got it," Alfie said as took his raspberries from the refrigerator. He poured them out into a bowl.

"Alfredo."

Alfie turned to see Monsieur DuBois.

"Before you begin, could you please give me your parents' number? I want to give them a call right away and let them know you and your sister are okay, especially with what's happened with your luggage." He held out a pen and paper.

With his teammates watching, Alfie took the paper and wrote down his parents' number. Only he accidentally-on-purpose wrote one digit wrong.

Soon the class was in the full swing of preparations. Jacques seasoned the meat, Madeline diced her vegetables, and Andre began the long task of making puff pastry from scratch. It involved rolling out the dough, folding it, and then refrigerating it for half an hour at a time, then repeating these steps seven more times.

For his part, Alfie was determined to follow every excruciating step of the raspberry-charlotte recipe Jacques had given him: baking the cake, making the sauce, letting it all cool, putting it together, and letting the cake refrigerate for hours. It would take a while, and he needed to pay close attention to each step, but Alfie was determined to get it all right.

"Jacques said this is his dad's recipe," Alfie said to Madeline as he worked. "You guys keep mentioning him. Does he cook, too, or something?"

"Well, of course," Madeline said. When Alfie gave her a curious look, she said, "His father is Jean-Luc Laurent."

"Okaaaay," Alfie said, confused.

"He's a really famous chef. He's won awards and cooked for kings and queens and celebrities," she said. "It's kind of a big deal that he gave you his father's recipe. If that thing comes out right," she said, "we'll win for sure."

"No pressure, huh?"

Madeline smiled. "We're all here to help."

Not long after, Alfie's cake was out of the oven, his sauce was off the stove, and they were both cooling on the counter. Andre's pastry was back in the refrigerator, setting. "I guess I can understand wanting to be the best," Alfie said.

Soon, the instructors called the students to dinner.

"Finally. I'm starving," Andre said. "Ugh, my pastry. It still needs one more roll out."

"I still have to put my cake together," Alfie said. "Want me to finish it for you?"

"Absolutely not!" Andre said. He thought for a moment. "But I am so hungry. Maybe just this once."

"No problem," Alfie said. *Ha! If Coach Schrader could see me now,* he thought, *being such a team player and all.*

"I'll ask Marcel if I can stay behind to finish up," Alfie said.

"Thanks, Alfie," Andre said.

Once he cleared it with Marcel and told Emilia that he was hanging behind, Alfie set to work finishing his cake while keeping an eye on the time so that he could also complete Andre's pastry.

Once everything was done he had to make room in the already-stuffed refrigerator. After lots of moving things out and aside and in and back out again, Alfie was exhausted from the day. As he left the kitchen for the evening, he even forgot to turn off the lights.

Chapter 14

The next morning, Alfie and the boys walked bleary-eyed down the stairs for breakfast. On the second-floor landing, they heard a piercing scream.

The boys rushed down toward the voice as Lardon the cat raced upstairs faster than they'd ever seen him go.

In the kitchen, they found a horrifying sight, which the other team—including Emilia—had already discovered.

"Our food!" gasped Jacques.

When Alfie had moved the dishes around to make room in the refrigerator, he'd accidentally left a few things out on the counter overnight. Andre's pastry dough, for one, sat there looking brown and squishy. Natalie's cake was a pile of crumbs, and Jacques's container of meat set in his marinade had fallen to the floor and broken open. Along the floor, identifying paw prints led the way out of the kitchen and up the stairs. Lardon had been there, licking and stepping in everything.

"My dish," Jacques said, picking up the beautiful steak he'd so carefully chosen at the market. "Who did this? How did this happen?"

"*Someone* left some of our stuff out on the counter overnight," Natalie said. Her arms were crossed tightly across her body—she looked wound up and ready for a fight.

"Who was the last one to leave the kitchen last night?" Emilia asked.

Andre looked at Alfie, waiting for him to answer.

"I, uh," Alfie began, "I stayed late to help finish some things."

Emilia looked at him the way their mom did when she was angry at him. He hated that look.

"Finish what things?" Natalie asked.

"My cake," Alfie answered.

Natalie looked inside the refrigerator. "Good news. Your cake is in perfect shape. Mine is ruined. Half our team's dishes are ruined!"

"I didn't mean to," Alfie said. "I'm sorry."

Alfie saw Jacques's accusing face and Emilia's disappointment, Andre's frustration, and Madeline's confusion, all aimed right at him. He couldn't remember a time when he felt worse.

"We can fix it," Alfie said to the team. "Maybe if we start now . . ."

"You know it takes all day," Andre said. "There's no time."

"We're disqualified," Jacques said. "There's no time to remake our food and no food to remake it with. It's over." Alfie thought he heard a quiver in his voice, which made him feel even worse.

"Come on, guys," Madeline said. "We can't give up so easily. Where's your sense of fight?"

Claudette, Natalie, and the others looked at one another. "If you want my opinion," Natalie said, "then I say I'm sorry, but it's a competition. Every man for himself."

"He's my brother," Emilia said. "I can't just pretend like he doesn't need help."

"But your own team needs help," Natalie said.

Claudette said, "Maybe Emilia's right. Besides, I want to win because my food is better, not because they don't have enough. Come on, Nat. Most of our dishes are okay, but all of theirs are pretty much ruined."

Natalie thought it over. "I don't know. I still think we should each make our own meals, but I guess since you're the captain, you can decide."

"Then I decide to help," Claudette said. "If Jacques's team agrees. What do you say?"

For a moment, the team didn't say anything. Finally, Jacques spoke up. "My father always says that you have to be flexible in the kitchen because something can always go wrong. I guess this is what he means. Let's do it."

The team captains shook on it. Alfie felt relieved that the competition was going on. Natalie, on the other hand, looked pretty annoyed. Alfie wondered if he'd feel the same way if he were in her place.

"Let's make the best meal the instructors have ever tasted," said Claudette.

"This will be as much fun as competing," Madeline said.

"But let's not tell the instructors," Claudette said. "You should never tell your guests the hardships you have to endure to prepare their meals."

"Agreed," Jacques said.

Everyone gathered around the prep tables and started the process of replanning the meals. Everyone piled their extra, unused ingredients onto the prep table to figure out who could use which scraps.

"How about a ratatouille for the main dish?" Andre said, looking at the donated ingredients from the girls.

"Okay," Jacques said. "I guess I can try."

"I need to redo my soup, but I can try something new," Madeline said. "Andre, we need something new to do with the sausages since the pastry is mush."

"I have an idea," Jacques said. "Why don't you have

sausage with chutney? I have a great recipe that has a little curry, some mango—it's really good. Want to try it?"

"Yeah, I could make that work," Andre said.

"Good thinking," Madeline said. "We just need a few ingredients from the market."

"Alfie, since your dish is safe why don't you go while we sort out the rest?" Jacques said.

"Okay," Alfie agreed.

"I'll go with you," Madeline offered. "I'll tell Marcel what's happening. He'll keep it a secret from the instructors for us."

"Good idea," Alfie said. "The last thing we need is a missing-persons alert."

Madeline giggled, but Alfie's own words gave him pause—Monsieur DuBois probably knew by now that the phone number Alfie gave him yesterday was wrong. He'd just have to deal with one crisis at a time. For now, nothing was more important than making sure his friends had a fair shot at serving the best meals of their lives.

Chapter 15

As they left the school, Alfie had another idea.

"Have you ever heard of the Rue Marche market?" he asked Madeline. It was the market Zia had mentioned at home. He couldn't believe he remembered the name.

"Sure," she said. "My grandmother used to take me there when I'd visit her as a kid. It's not far from here. Should we go?"

"Yeah, let's try it. Maybe it'll have some different things that'll inspire us."

That was one reason to try the market, but the other reason was Zia. Going there just might help give their dishes that little bit of magic they needed before being served to a great Parisian chef.

As Madeline led the way he said, "Thanks for not being mad at me. I feel pretty dumb about what I did."

"Why should I be mad? It was an easy mistake," she said. "You were just so focused on making a great cake and it had been a long day."

Alfie knew she was just being nice. "Uh-huh, sure. But leaving food out is more like a stupid mistake."

"We've all done it before," she said, finally cracking a smile.

"Yeah, right."

Once they'd gotten everything they needed, they headed back to the school. Alfie even  impressed Madeline by leading the way.

The kitchen was in full swing when they walked in. Emilia helped Andre with his chutney while Claudette helped with the ratatouille and Natalie put the finishing touches on her team's dishes, including roasted chicken and carrots, garlic mushrooms, and mini quiche starters.

"Thirty minutes left!" called Jacques, and everyone moved in a mad scramble to finish before time was called. Everything was going according to plan—the food tasted great, and all the dishes were almost finished. Alfie couldn't believe they'd pulled it off—but they had!

Until Monsieur DuBois appeared in the kitchen's doorway.

"Alfredo and Emilia Bertolizzi!"

All movement in the kitchen came to a complete stop.

"I need to see you both in my office *immediately!*"

Alfie felt the bottom of his stomach drop out. It was finally over. They were busted. What was going to happen to them? One look at his sister's face and Alfie knew she was as scared as he was.

Alfie put down the spoon he'd been using to drizzle raspberry sauce over the top of the finished cake. He and Emilia started toward the door.

"Monsieur DuBois!" said Madame Rousseau just behind him in the doorway. "He's here! Chef Orleans has arrived!"

Monsieur DuBois turned quickly from the students. "Already? Has he asked for me yet? Did you seat him in the parlor? Did you offer him a drink?"

"Yes, yes, yes!" Madame Rousseau said.

"Get this kitchen in order!" he said to the students. "It's time for the dinner!" He dashed off so quickly to meet the guest of honor that he actually tripped over his own feet, making the students giggle.

"He ran out of here like his pants were on fire," Madeline said with a laugh.

It was controlled chaos as they prepped their dishes. Every part of every dish was carefully arranged on the platters, just like they'd learned to do in class. All the students had tasted the food and knew it would impress everyone. The only thing they couldn't taste was Alfie's cake, since it had to be cut and served at the table.

The students lined up as Chef Orleans and the
instructors headed into the dining room. Chef Orleans
towered over Monsieur DuBois, dressed in a crisp,
starched white shirt, dark jeans, and a blue blazer. He
had salt-and-pepper hair and an amused look on his
face. Alfie didn't know if it was from watching Monsieur
DuBois fall all over himself or because he was about to eat
food prepared by a bunch of kids.

Finally they were sent back to the kitchen to wait for their food to be eaten.

"I wonder what they're saying," Andre whispered nervously. "Do you think they can tell what was made at the last minute?"

"No way," said Emilia. "Everything tasted as if it took days to make."

After what felt like hours of waiting, Madame Rousseau finally called them into the dining room.

"Students, we were more than impressed with the food you put before us today," Madame Rousseau began. "We know this was a lot to ask of such young students, but we did it because we knew you were up for the challenge. You certainly did not disappoint us. Congratulations on a job well done."

The instructors and guest gave the students a hearty round of applause, which made Alfie and the rest of the students feel amazing.

"Only I know which meal was created by which team,"

Madame Rousseau continued. "So the judges do not know who made what. Chef Orleans, would you like to announce the winner?"

Chef Orleans stood from his seat at the table. "First I would like to say thank you all for having me, and thank you to the students for creating such fine food for us today. You all deserve a round of applause." The students clapped for their teammates, and it was clear that the race to win the dinner was a close one.

"But I must say," Chef Orleans continued, "that although both meals were extraordinary, I like to always remember that sometimes the best foods are the simplest ones, the meals that let the natural ingredients shine on their own. That is why we have decided to award the dinner to . . . the meal with the extraordinary ratatouille."

Jacques's team! Alfie and his teammates couldn't help themselves—they jumped and cheered and congratulated one another. Alfie was relieved he hadn't made his team lose—but having his team win meant Emilia's team lost.

Her dream of eating a fancy dinner in the Eiffel Tower was over.

She tried to act like it was no big deal, but Alfie knew she was crushed.

He leaned toward her and said, "I'll ask if I can give you my place."

Finally, Jacques stepped forward to speak for his team. "We just want to say we had a lot of fun making the meal, and I know you're not supposed to tell your guests the trouble you've been through, but I think my team will agree . . . ," he said, turning to the team, who all nodded for Jacques to go ahead. "We had some . . . problems with our foods this morning, but everyone worked together to complete and even re-create a lot of the dishes. We just don't think we should win the prize alone, and we know that everyone can't go, so . . . as great as the dinner sounds, we'd rather stay here with the other team. If that's okay."

The adults all looked at one another.

"I must say," Monsieur DuBois said. "I'm very

surprised, and impressed. We had no idea that there was any drama in the kitchen. Chef Orleans?" Monsieur DuBois, Madame Rousseau, and Chef Orleans put their heads together and quietly discussed what to do among themselves. "Since these are such unusual circumstances, I'm afraid we have to amend our original winners of the top prize, although you should all be very proud of your work. With that said, the team who will be going to dinner at Le Jules Verne," he said, "is . . . *both* teams!"

Now the students really erupted into cheers. Everyone won!

"A quick phone call to the chef and maître d'," Chef Orleans said, "and all will be worked out."

The students raced upstairs to change for dinner. Jacques and Andre loaned Alfie some of their clothes.

"Thanks," Alfie told them, pulling on Jacques's shirt.

"Looks like you're going to make it through the whole week without having your luggage," Jacques said.

"Yeah, it's weird the airline hasn't even called," Andre said.

"And what was all that about Monsieur DuBois wanting to see you and your sister?"

"I don't know," Alfie said. "Maybe the airline *did* call."

"It didn't seem like he had any good news. He seemed pretty mad," Andre said as they started downstairs. "If I were you, I'd steer clear of him tonight."

"Good idea," Alfie said.

As the class headed out into the cool Parisian night, Alfie and Emilia stayed in the back of the pack, far away from Monsieur DuBois.

Chapter 16

The view was unlike anything they'd ever seen. The beauty of Paris they'd seen all week, walking the streets, eating in the restaurants and cafés, and shopping in the markets, became a picture before them, as they sat high above the city at a table inside the Eiffel Tower.

They'd arrived at the restaurant via private elevator, and the students and instructors—including Chef Orleans—were escorted inside to a large table along the window. Through the iron latticework of the tower they looked down at the twinkling lights of the city.

Le Jules Verne served all kinds of elegant food. It was different from the big portions of food Alfie and

Emilia were used to getting at home, though. They were served five different courses—five!—which included an appetizer, soup, salad, the main course, and dessert.

Alfie really couldn't believe they'd all pulled together to create—or rather, *re*-create—such a spectacular meal for Chef Orleans. Even though they'd been rushed and stressed while making it, Alfie realized that they'd also had a lot of fun working together. He wondered if that's what Coach Schrader had been talking about all along.

As they worked their way through a decadent dessert of spicy chocolate sorbet, Alfie noticed that Emilia had fallen quiet. She sat with one hand on her spoon and the other resting under her chin as she stared out at the twinkling city lights.

"Are you okay?" he asked her. When she looked at him, Alfie realized she had tears in her eyes. "Emilia! What's wrong?"

She swirled her spoon in melting sorbet. "I was just thinking how it looks like we're going to be here another night. I love it here, and I really like my new friends." She looked down the table at Madeline, Claudette, and Natalie, who were arguing with the boys over what was better—sorbet or gelato. "But I was thinking how I'm not going to sleep in my bed *again* tonight. And I miss Mom and Dad and Zia and my friends back home. Is that lame?"

"No," Alfie said, because he was starting to feel the same way, too. "We'll go home tonight."

"But how?"

"Remember—the omelet at the café?"

"Do you really think it'll work?" Emilia asked.

"Sure, why not? I even have some money left over from the market, so we don't have to worry about that. We don't have to worry about anything," Alfie said, like he had it all figured out. Truthfully, he had no idea if it'd work, or even if it had almost worked in the first place. Maybe his stomach had just been upset, or he'd been excited about the day's activities. It could have been lots of things.

A clinking noise turned their attention to the end of the table, where Jacques stood with his water glass.

"To our new American friends, Alfie and Emilia," he said. "For messing things up, then making them better than before."

"Hear, hear!" the group agreed.

Alfie and Emilia blushed. They raised their glasses with their new friends to toast all the work they'd done together.

As they got into the elevator to leave, Alfie and Emilia were nervous and unsure about what would happen next.

"Why so quiet?" Madeline asked them as the elevator raced down.

Emilia said, "I'm just really going to miss you guys, that's all."

"We'll keep in touch," she said. "Oh, that reminds me. I made you both something." As the elevator doors opened and the class filed out, Madeline handed them each something small wrapped in wax paper. "Madeleines!" she said. "You know, the cookie?" Alfie unwrapped his and found a small shell-shaped cookie. "I made them earlier today for everyone. You're probably too full to have it now, but save it for later. And maybe sometime," she added, glancing at Alfie, "you can make us some homemade Alfredo sauce."

Alfie smiled. "Definitely."

The students walked together back to the school, talking about the day ahead and how they would all keep in touch once the course ended. Andre dared Jacques to jump onto his back for a piggyback ride, and Jacques took the dare. Andre stumbled a few steps while the class cheered him on but finally had to dump Jacques—who made a dramatic fall to the ground.

"Monsieur DuBois!" called Madeline. The adults walked behind the students, keeping an eye on them. "Can we please make hot chocolate in the kitchen and stay up for just a little bit?"

Everyone started walking backward and begging, "Pleeaase!"

"Absolutely not," he said. "You know you all have a strict curfew."

The class continued to beg, and Monsieur DuBois finally gave in. Everyone cheered.

When they arrived back at the school, everyone raced

toward the kitchen—hot chocolate, Alfie and Emilia knew, might also offer a way home. They thought they could at least give it a shot before heading to the omelet café.

The kids dashed to the pantry and refrigerators. Claudette and Natalie grabbed flour, sugar, chocolate, and other ingredients.

"Let's make cookies, too," Claudette said as Jacques started on the hot chocolate.

"I know this really good chocolate cookie recipe that I just learned to make," Andre said.

"Don't forget the sugar," Claudette said. She opened the container, scooped out a teaspoon, and flicked it onto his head.

Everyone paused for a moment, waiting to see what Andre would do. In a flash, he grabbed a huge handful of flour and said, "You're going to get it now!" and tossed it at Claudette.

"FOOD FIGHT!" someone yelled, and it was on. Suddenly flour and sugar drifted through the air like a snowy mist. Alfie grabbed several marshmallows and pelted Emilia in the head before ducking behind a large soup pot beneath the prep table. His sister launched an egg at him like a seasoned baseball player. Alfie turned his back just in time, and it slammed onto his shoulder blade, a splat catching on his chin.

After several days of working so hard, learning as much as they could about French food, and experiencing total sensory overload while seeing all the sights of Paris, it felt great to just let go and act wild. Alfie raced toward Madeline with a handful of sugar, but she saw him coming. They pelted each other at the same time, laughing so hard Alfie could taste the sugar in the back of his throat.

"What is this! What is going on!" They were not questions—they were angry exclamations coming from a red-faced Monsieur DuBois, who stood in the doorway of the kitchen. Madame Rousseau stood behind him. She looked shocked—but her mouth revealed a tiny hint of a smile, Alfie thought.

"Clean up this mess immediately. And you two,"
Monsieur DuBois said, pointing to Alfie and Emilia.
"Come with me."

Alfie dusted the flour, sugar, and eggshells off himself
as best as he could. As he and Emilia started out of the
kitchen, Madeline whispered, "Good luck."

Alfie and Emilia stepped inside Monsieur DuBois's office and sat at the chairs in front of his desk.

"Are you ready to tell us what is going on?" he said. Alfie, panicking, decided not speaking was the best thing to do until his mind worked again and he came up with a plan.

"You are not enrolled in this school," Monsieur DuBois stated plainly. "We are not sure how you came to be here, where your family is, or what they know, but we do know that you cannot stay here a moment longer. Alfredo," he continued, "I think you know that the phone number you gave me was incorrect. Am I right?"

Alfie looked down at his hands. "Yes, sir."

Monsieur DuBois sighed. "I have to say, you have both been good students. But I do not know what this charade is you are playing. Have you run away from home?"

"No, not exactly," Alfie said.

"I need to contact your parents right away. That, or the authorities," he said. "I suggest you give me the correct phone number. In the meantime, Madame Rousseau will escort you both into the lounge, where you will sit and await further instructions."

They followed her to the cozy den, where Lardon sat licking his paw and cleaning his face. Madame Rousseau stepped outside, and Alfie and Emilia finally had a moment alone.

"Alfie, what are we going to do?" Emilia asked. "Do you think he can actually call Mom and Dad? Will that work?"

"I don't know," Alfie said.

"What if we have to go to jail? What if we're sent to an orphanage or something?" Emilia said, the panic in her voice rising.

"Let me think for a minute." Alfie could just hear Monsieur DuBois and Madame Rousseau in the other room.

"Is it going through?" Madame Rousseau asked. Alfie leaned forward and saw Monsieur DuBois with the phone to his ear. He shook his head no. So for some reason, they couldn't call his parents.

"Well, I suppose we should call the police," Madame Rousseau said. "We can't just let them leave without supervision. They must have run away."

"Alfie," Emilia said. "What should we do?"

"Yes, this is Monsieur DuBois over at the Young Chefs School of Fine French Cooking," they heard him say into the phone. "Unfortunately we have two American children who we believe have run away from home. Could you send someone over?"

Alfie knew the instructors would soon be back in the room, watching them closely until the authorities arrived. He had to think of something fast, so he did the only thing that came to mind.

"Run!" he said, grabbing Emilia by the wrist and tugging her out of the room and toward the front door.

Madame Rousseau heard the commotion and quickly ran out of the office toward them. "Children! Wait!"

Alfie and Emilia dashed out the front door and ran as fast as they could manage. Alfie looked closely at street signs and the businesses he recognized as they whizzed by, trying to get them where he knew they needed to go while escaping from Madame Rousseau.

"Where are we going?" Emilia yelled from beside him as they ran.

"The omelet café." That had to be the answer, since Alfie was sure he'd almost gone home that day with Jacques and Andre.

After several turns and two stretches down long avenues, they had lost Madame Rousseau. Down the street, Alfie spotted the fountain he remembered the café being across from and then the red awning of Café Bertrand. They finally slowed down, walking the last half block.

"Are you okay?" he asked Emilia as they both panted, trying to catch their breath. Alfie hadn't run that fast since he was last on the soccer field several days ago. He wasn't sure how much, if any, time had passed at home since they left. But knew they needed to get back.

"I'm fine," Emilia said, looking down the street to make sure no one was following them. Once they'd calmed down she said, "I feel like a bank robber or something!"

Alfie smiled. "A bank robber dressed as a cake. You've got flour all in your hair."

She dusted out her hair and said, "You've got egg on your face."

Alfie felt crusted egg on his jaw. They had cleaned themselves up as best they could when Alfie noticed that their situation had gotten even worse.

"Wait a minute," he said, looking across the street. The café—it was dark. He raced over with Emilia behind him. When they got to the door they read the notice:

CLOSED FOR THE EVENING FOR A PRIVATE EVENT.

Alfie's heart sank. He leaned his head against the locked door. Now what would they do?

"Oh no," Emilia said. "Maybe we should go get some

hot chocolate somewhere? Or sneak back into the school tonight and figure it out?"

"No, no," Alfie said. He was beyond frustrated and had no idea what to do next. "We can't go back to the school and we've had hot chocolate enough times here to know that won't work." So where would they sleep tonight? On the streets? In some alley?

"Let's just stay calm and think about it," Emilia said. Alfie was glad she wasn't panicking. He didn't think he could handle it if she had a breakdown right now. "Oh! Hey, look!" Out of her pocket she pulled the madeleines Madeline had given them. "At least we won't starve."

Alfie took the cookie from her while his mind raced with possibilities of how this night would end. None of them were good.

He bit into the soft, blond cookie, which had a slight vanilla taste.

"It's good," Emilia said. "Reminds me of my birthday cake this year."

"That was a good one," Alfie said. "If only you'd picked a better birthday dinner."

"Hey, how was I supposed to know we'd all get food poisoning!" she said.

"I wonder if I'll be spending my next birthday in Paris," Alfie said, even though his birthday was months away.

"Not even funny," Emilia said.

"You! Children!" A voice filled the street, echoing off the buildings. A police officer. "Stay right where you are!"

"Uh-oh! We've been found!" Alfie popped the last of the madeleine into this mouth as he and Emilia grabbed each other's hands and dashed down the street. And as they did, Alfie felt a shift in the air.

Chapter 17

It was another dark morning in a cold room and the smell of freshly baked bread filled Alfie's nose. He got out of bed and walked on bare feet across the cold floor, but this time the view was different. It was a yard. *His* yard.

Alfie burst out of the room and ran into the hall, where he found Emilia. They literally started jumping up and down with joy. They were home!

Dad scooted past them in the hall, yawning loudly. "You two sure are excited that it's Saturday."

It was Saturday—which meant that Alfie hadn't missed his soccer game!

In the kitchen stood Zia—wonderful, lovely Zia. Alfie

only now realized how much he'd missed her. She pulled a baking sheet out of the oven, and on it were golden, puffy, delicate French croissants. Mom sat at the island sipping coffee as Dad poured himself a cup.

"Zia, you're going all-out today," Mom said. "Morning, kids."

"Oh, I just thought I'd make a fun breakfast from my days in Paris," Zia said, her signature sneaky glance aimed directly at Alfie and Emilia.

"The kids need protein, too," Mom said. "I'll scramble a couple of eggs. Alfie will need the extra energy for his big game today."

"My game," Alfie said, remembering he wasn't actually *playing* in the game. For a moment he'd managed to forget. At least this meant he wasn't going to be kicked off the team. "You mean my new position of keeping the bench warm for the other players."

"A very important job!" Zia said. Alfie wasn't sure if she was teasing or if she just didn't get it.

But Alfie was starting to get it. He remembered the kitchen in Paris and how they'd all rallied together to make an incredible meal. He remembered how no job was too small—even the simple task of washing the vegetables was essential when time was so important.

"You're right, Zia," Alfie said. "I guess I'll go out there and be the very best benchwarmer Coach Schrader has ever seen."

That afternoon, he did just that—with his family

cheering for him from the stands.

"Let's go, guys, you got this!" Alfie cheered, handing out water to the players who came off the field. He kept it cold and at the ready, the best water boy the team had ever seen. "Jackson, you're doing awesome on the goal. Watch out for that fullback—he keeps trying to sneak into your right corner."

"Thanks, Alfie," Jackson said, taking a squeeze of water from one of the bottles.

"Good job, Bertolizzi," Coach Schrader said as the boys ran back out onto the field. "I might have to promote you to manager."

"Coach, I really think I could make a great captain, if only I could play—"

"Relax." Coach smiled. "I'm only teasing. You've done a great job. Keep it up and this game is ours."

They did win. Jackson kept his eyes on that right pocket and prevented the Thunderbirds from scoring a winning goal. Alfie joined as the team celebrated the victory. In the stands, his family cheered along with the other parents.

"You did a great job," Emilia told him.

Alfie smiled. "Thanks."

"You must be starved," Zia said, coming over to them. "All that hard work. Here, have a bite." She held out the plastic container of the food that she'd been sharing with others in the bleachers during the game.

"What is it?" Alfie asked, inspecting the half-moon pieces of what looked like stuffed pasta.

"They're called pot stickers," Zia said. "Chinese dumplings. I made them from a recipe I learned in Hong Kong. They're filled with pork and vegetables, and then I fried them. A perfect postgame snack for such a great player."

Alfie took a pot sticker as Zia watched him closely. "Hong Kong, huh?"

A Note from Giada

My grandmother used to tell me beautiful stories about her time in Paris as a glamorous movie actress. She painted a picture of the city's elegance and sophistication, and I couldn't wait to explore it myself. I was lucky enough to go to culinary school in Paris, and the moment I set foot in the city, my grandmother's words came rushing back to me.

For nearly a thousand years, Paris has been one of the most important cities in Europe for arts and sciences, and today it is home to hundreds of galleries and museums. And from the Eiffel Tower to Notre Dame to the Arc de Triomphe, Paris probably has more familiar landmarks than any other city in the world, and they make the city both magical and grand.

But what Paris is also known for—and why I fell in love with it— is its food: the pastries, the bread, the cheese, the chocolate, and so much more.

Although I'm no longer able to listen to my grandmother's stories of Paris, I'm so happy that I can share her memories of that enchanting city, as well as my own, with my daughter.

Xo

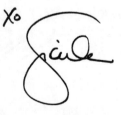